Stand Up for Citizenship
Growing Character

By Frank Murphy

21st Century
Junior Library

Published in the United States of America by
Cherry Lake Publishing
Ann Arbor, Michigan
www.cherrylakepublishing.com

Reading Adviser: Marla Conn, MS, Ed., Literacy specialist, Read-Ability, Inc.

Photo Credits: ©Rawpixel.com/Shutterstock, cover, 1; ©siam.pukkato/Shutterstock, 4; ©Phuong D. Nguyen/Shutterstock, 6; ©Aleksandra Suzi /Shutterstock, 8; © Rawpixel.com /Shutterstock, 10; ©XiXinXing/Shutterstock, 12; ©Brocreative/ Shutterstock, 14; ©Rob Crandall/Shutterstock, 16; ©Rachael Warriner/Shutterstock, 18; ©zenstock/Shutterstock, 20

Library of Congress Cataloging-in-Publication Data

Names: Murphy, Frank, 1966- author.
Title: Stand up for citizenship / written by Frank Murphy.
Description: Ann Arbor, Michigan : Cherry Lake Publishing, 2019. | Series:
    Growing character | Includes bibliographical references and index. |
    Audience: K to grade 3.
Identifiers: LCCN 2019007377 | ISBN 9781534147416 (hardcover) | ISBN
    9781534148840 (pdf) | ISBN 9781534150270 (pbk.) | ISBN 9781534151703
    (hosted ebook)
Subjects: LCSH: Citizenship—Juvenile literature. | Conduct of life—Juvenile
    literature.
Classification: LCC JF801 .M867 2019 | DDC 323.6/5—dc23
LC record available at https://lccn.loc.gov/2019007377

Cherry Lake Publishing would like to acknowledge the work of The Partnership for 21st Century Skills.
Please visit *www.p21.org* for more information.

Printed in the United States of America
Corporate Graphics

CONTENTS

Always throw your trash in a garbage or recycling bin.

What Is Citizenship?

Pearl and Emma were walking down the street. An empty water bottle was on the ground. Pearl picked it up and put it in the **recycling** bin.

"Why did you pick that up?" asked Emma. "It wasn't yours."

Pearl answered, "Because it's litter. A good **citizen** doesn't let litter stay on the ground."

Good citizens keep their yards, streets, and parks clean so their community will look nice.

A good citizen helps make their surroundings a better place. Your family, your school, and your neighborhood are part of your surroundings. All of these are part of your **community**. In fact, the entire world is one big community. Good citizens are aware that what they do **affects** others in their communities.

Look!

Look around your neighborhood. Do you see any ways that you could help your neighbors?

Recycling and composting your trash is a way you can be a good citizen and do your part in solving a big problem.

Being a Good Citizen

There are many ways to be a good citizen. Pearl does chores at home. She recycles bottles, cans, and paper at home and at school. In her neighborhood, she cleans up after her dog. Her actions show that she cares about others and the places she's a part of. Her actions show that she is a **responsible** citizen.

There are many benefits to planting trees. How many can you think of?

You can be a good citizen in other ways too. You can **volunteer** with a group to help clean a park. You can ask permission from adults to help plant a tree in a public space. You can help support an organization in your community by raising money for it. All of these things will help the whole community.

Create!

Sit down with your family to make a list of the ways you can help your community. Think of things your neighbors, public library, or school might need. Put the list in a spot where you and your family will see it often. Try to do at least one thing on the list each week.

Try to make new students feel welcome at your school.

Another way to show good citizenship is to try and make your school a better place. If you see something that needs to be fixed, let your teacher or principal know.

A new student joined Emma's class. She made sure he felt welcome by eating lunch with him. She also asked if he needed help during the day.

Being a good citizen means taking care of the places and the people surrounding you.

Try to stay on sidewalks instead of walking in people's yards.

Obeying laws is another way to be a good citizen. Damaging or stealing someone else's property is against the law. So is not following traffic rules. Tell an adult if you see someone breaking the law. This helps keep your community safe from crime.

Ask Questions!

Write down two rules you must follow at home. Then ask a friend the rules they must follow at home. Were there any rules your friends named that were the same?

When your parents or grandparents go to vote, ask if you can join them. You may get the chance to walk into a voting booth and see how voting works. You'll be voting one day too!

Spreading Citizenship

Really good citizens learn about and stay aware of what is happening in their community and their world. Pearl and her brother, Will, talk to their parents and watch news programs to learn about **candidates** who are running for office. They aren't old enough to vote yet. But one day they will be. By learning now how leaders are elected, they will be better citizens when they are adults.

Learn about your local and state leaders. It will help you know more about what is going on in your community and the world.

Pearl once wrote a letter to her local **congresswoman**. Pearl told her how her neighborhood park needed more trash cans and signs about cleaning up after pets. Pearl asked for help. Her congresswoman wrote back! And eventually, the park received more trash cans and signs. Later, the congresswoman came to Pearl's school to thank Pearl for making her aware of the problem at the park.

Following the rules makes the world a safer place for everyone.

Think about the places you go and the people you spend time with. Show good citizenship! Do your part to make the world better. You should follow the rules. You might plant a tree. You could help a classmate. You may write a letter. All of your actions can help others become better citizens.

Everything good citizens do makes an **impact** on the world.

GLOSSARY

affects (uh-FEKTS) changes someone or something

candidates (KAN-dih-dates) people who are running in an election

citizen (SIT-ih-zuhn) a person who lives in a certain town or city, state or nation

community (kuh-MYOO-nih-tee) a group of people living in the same place

congresswoman (KAHNG-gris-wum-uhn) a female member of Congress, which is the lawmaking body of the United States

impact (IM-pakt) have a strong effect on someone or something

recycling (ree-SYE-kuhl-ing) collecting used items that can be made into new products

responsible (rih-SPAHN-suh-buhl) feeling a sense of duty to do something, care for someone, or take charge of something

volunteer (vah-luh-TEER) offer to do a job for no pay

FIND OUT MORE

BOOKS

Eggers, Dave. *What Can a Citizen Do?* San Francisco, CA: Chronicle Books, 2018.

Small, Mary. *Being a Good Citizen*. Minneapolis, MN: Picture Window Books, 2006.

Suen, Anastasia. *Vote for Isaiah! A Citizenship Story*. Edina, MN: Magic Wagon, 2009.

WEBSITES

PBS Kids—You Choose
https://pbskids.org/youchoose
Watch videos and do activities that help you learn more about presidents and elections.

KidsHealth—Be a Volunteer
http://kidshealth.org/kid/feeling/thought/volunteering.html
Learn more about volunteering.

INDEX

ABOUT THE AUTHOR

Frank Murphy has written several books for young readers. They are about famous people, historical events, and leadership. He was born in California but now lives in Pennsylvania with his family. Frank tries to be a good citizen by volunteering with organizations that help veterans.